Dedicated to all Women Leading Authentic Lives

Grandma Loves Her Harley Too

Nancy Vogl & David Strange

Illustrated by Nichoel Gibson

Cherry Tree Press

Traverse City, Michigan

In the summertime, when visiting her grandpa and grandma at their cottage, Chelsea likes waking up in the early morning hours just as the sun rises over the lake. Looking out at the still, blue water, she gets excited thinking about all the fun she's going to have outside... swimming, fishing with Grandpa, and looking for beautiful stones on the shore.

Chelsea also has fun helping her grandma. Sometimes they go shopping, or they dust the house while listening to great music, or they might bake something yummy, like cherry pie! But more than anything, Chelsea loves just being with her grandma and talking about all kinds of things.

One day, while helping Grandma in the garden, Chelsea spied a purple
motorcycle by the garage, and asked, "Grandma, whose bike is that?"

Grandma replied, "Why, it's mine, of course,
and just like Grandpa's bike, it's a Harley!"

Startled, Chelsea said, "What?! Grandma, I didn't know you rode a motorcycle too. Wow!"
Then puzzled, Chelsea asked, "But why? Aren't you scared to ride it?
Besides that, you're a girl…you're a grandma, for goodness sakes!"

"Why, Chelsea Marie! I can't believe you said that. And, of course I'm not scared.
Just because I'm a girl doesn't mean I wouldn't love riding a motorcycle
just like Grandpa, just like your dad…just like lots of people, men *and* women.
And I have lots of reasons why I love riding my new Harley."

I do a lot to take care of the people I love, your grandpa, my children and grandchildren. I take care of the house, I work hard at my job, and I volunteer my time to help other people. My life is very busy! It took me a long time to realize I need to take care of me too. One of the things I do for myself is to climb on my Harley and just ride.

As soon as I get on the road, I feel like
I've "escaped" and I just breathe. I breathe
in the fresh air and simply enjoy the scenery,
appreciating every single moment and the
time I have to myself.

I always discover something that makes
me so glad I'm riding my motorcycle.

Like coming up over a hill and finding a spectacular sight in front of me. It's as if I were handed a beautiful present.

And the solitude of an open road gives me time to think. I feel guided, no matter what is going on in my life. I remember to believe in who I am and that I can accomplish whatever it is I put my mind to.

But riding my Harley is also a great adventure and lots of fun! I've been to some amazing places and had more freedom because I was on my motorcycle.

It's also wonderful riding with my friends. Sometimes we take off and don't have any plans on where we're going. We just explore, taking back roads, finding lots of surprises along the way.

We love riding through small, quaint towns.

Sometimes we stop for lunch, or do a little shopping, or just pass through. Whatever we do, we just have a good time.

One of the things I love most about riding a Harley
is how wonderful it is to get together at all kinds of
events with other people who ride Harleys too.

Harley riders are the most generous people in the world! They're always doing something to help people in need. We meet to "ride," raising money to help them. It makes me happy when I'm doing something good for others, especially children who might be sick or disabled.

When I'm on my Harley, my problems just seem to drift away.
I see things more clearly. I'm more inspired. I feel renewed, giving me
more energy to take care of everyone and everything else in my life.

Chelsea, I have lots of reasons why I ride. Sometimes riding my Harley feels like a great big celebration! I'm reminded of all I have to be grateful for…and that includes you. So, now do you see why I love riding my Harley so much?"

Chelsea nodded, but she was deep in thought, imagining what it would be like to ride a Harley. Then, suddenly, it hit her what Grandma was really saying to her.

"Grandma, you're always teaching me something!" Chelsea paused, and a smile spread across her face. "I know I'll have a lot of responsibilities someday too, and if I take care of me, I'll be able to love everyone else even more. And if I believe in myself I'll be able to accomplish all kinds of things. But there's one more thing I think you forgot to say, something I know is true of you."

"What's that Chelsea?"

"Most importantly, Grandma, just like you, more than anything…"

"I've got to be me!"

If you would like additional copies of this book, please visit:
www.CherryTreePress.com
or inquire at your local Harley dealership